Springtime Discovery

The Tara Chadwick Series

Springtime Discovery

Jerry B. Jenkins

MOODY PRESS
CHICAGO

Scripture quotations are from *The Living Bible.*

ISBN: 0-8024-8542-1

1 2 3 4 5 6 Printing/LC/Year 94 93 92 91 90

Printed in the United States of America

To the readers
of the Dallas O'Neil and the Baker Street Sports Club series
and the Dallas O'Neil Mysteries
who were kind enough
to let me know
that you enjoyed them

Contents

GATE
43
SAIR

1

Leaving

As she and her mother hurried through the Milwaukee airport, Tara Chadwick pressed her lips together. Her breath came in short bursts as she fought the tears. As usual, her mother didn't notice.

"You're going to have a good time, Tara," Mrs. Chadwick said, reaching to run a hand through her daughter's short blond hair. Tara hated when she did that but didn't have the energy to pull away. "And don't worry about that softball team. You're only going to miss two games."

Tara wanted to tell her mother that it wasn't the games she was worried about, but right now her mother was doing more talking than listening.

"I've got to pick up Ray after school so he can get his paper route done before Jeff's track meet tonight. You know Ray's the only fourth grade paper boy in town."

Tara sighed. She knew. It seemed being the best or the only or the tallest or the handsomest was all her mother cared about. "Yeah, and Jeff's the youngest runner on the varsity track team," Tara said, surprised at how unsteady her voice was. She was going to break down and sob, she just knew it.

Her mother looked at her watch. "I've got twenty minutes before I have to get back to the bank," she said. "I can stay with you almost until you board."

Tara was grateful for that. She didn't want to leave. She wondered why Ray and Jeff got to stay home over spring break and she had to be shipped off to her aunt and uncle's. But she had asked so many times and had argued with her mother so often that she knew it was hopeless to bring it up again.

Her mother steered her toward the security check, and as she followed Tara through she called out, "I swear you're taller than I am, honey. You have to be the tallest girl in the sixth grade."

Tara nodded. Who cared? She was taller than all the boys too, but it didn't matter. She was the best athlete and the fastest runner too, but that meant a lot more to her mother than it did to her. The other tall girl in the class, her best friend, Suzanne Yorty, hated her height and always slouched, trying to hide it. Tara would never do that. She was trim and in shape with long, powerful but not muscly legs. Her height didn't bother her.

Neither did her looks. She was grateful to have smooth, clear skin, but she wondered how long it would last. Jeff's face erupted when he was in eighth grade, and she figured hers would too.

But none of that made any difference. The only thing she cared about was that something awful had happened to her family. She didn't fully understand it and doubted she ever would, but what she did know she didn't like.

Clarice Chadwick slid her daughter's ticket across the counter. "She has a prearranged seat, and her aunt will meet her at the other end," she said.

"A window seat," the agent said. "She's not under thirteen, is she?"

"Turned twelve last week," Mrs. Chadwick said. "Tallest in her class."

Tara cringed.

"And such a pretty girl," the agent added, turning to Tara. "If for any reason your aunt is not there to meet you, let someone from the airline know immediately, OK?"

Tara nodded. She hated being treated like a child, but she felt more like a child just then than she had for years.

Her mother checked her watch again. "It looks like your plane is here, but we can sit for a while."

They sat in a large, circular room where they could see several gates at once. At one people were boarding. Another was empty. At another, passengers streamed in from the plane, greeting loved ones. Tara put her carry-on bag on her lap and studied it to keep from having to return her mother's gaze.

"Don't worry about us," Mrs. Chadwick said. "We'll be fine."

That was a laugh. Tara was ready to explode, and her mother thought she was worried about her mother and two brothers. Tara shook her head. "I know *you'll* be fine," she said. "What about Dad?"

Mrs. Chadwick stiffened and crossed her legs. "Your dad," she said, "couldn't be happier. He's got his girl friend, and he's forced me to work, and he doesn't take any responsibility for you and the boys anymore."

Tara didn't know why she chose to react to the least troubling part of her mother's attack when it was her dad's absence she really wanted to talk about. But she said, "Mother, you've been working at the bank for years."

Her mother leaned forward. "You know as well as I do, young lady, that I worked because I wanted to. I worked because we like some of the nicer things in life. You never complained about my working when we went to Disneyworld or the Grand Canyon or Niagara Falls, did you?"

"Dad made enough money."

"You father makes plenty of money, but the kinds of cars he likes and the—oh, Tara, do we have to go through this again? He's happy, and if I never see him again, it will be too soon."

"I don't want you to get a divorce," Tara said, finally breaking down. She had said that over and over during the last month, and that, she knew, was why her mother was sending her away for spring break.

Mrs. Chadwick touched Tara's shoulder, but Tara could tell it was more from embarrassment than from trying to comfort her. Her mother leaned close to shield her from anyone else's view. "Come on, come on, Tara, don't do this now. You'll be boarding in a few minutes."

Tara looked into her mother's face and forced herself to speak through her quiet sobs. "I don't want you to get a divorce!"

Her mother frowned and sat back. "It's a little too late for that. You know it's only a matter of time."

"But you can stop it," Tara said, not sure she was right.

"Oh, honey, if I stopped it, your father would file for divorce. There's going to be an end to this already dead marriage no matter what I do. We both want this divorce, and the sooner the better."

Mrs. Chadwick fished in her purse for a tissue and thrust it into Tara's hand. Rather than dab at her eyes, Tara unfolded the tissue and pressed it over her whole face. "I don't believe you," she said.

She knew her mother heard her muffled comment, but Mrs. Chadwick said nothing. Tara pulled the paper away from her face and said it again. "I don't believe you."

Clearly, her mother had heard enough. She leaned forward and spoke directly into Tara's ear, and Tara could imagine what she looked like. When she was angry, her mother's face seemed more pointed than ever, her short, thin nose piercing the air, her dark eyes narrowed and blazing.

"I am not going to discuss this with you again," Mrs. Chadwick said. "We have been over it and over it, and I'm sick of it. I know you long to remember your father as a man who loved you and the rest of us, but the fact is he has dragged us through the dirt, humiliated and made a fool of me, and I'm as happy to see him gone as he is to be gone."

Tara had learned not to argue with her mother when she had this tone, but she couldn't help herself. She had the sinking feeling that once she was in line to get on that airplane, she would lose whatever hope she had for getting her parents back together. And so she repeated herself again. "I don't believe you."

Her mother took a deep breath, looking exasperated. "Just what is it you don't believe? Do you really think I would take your father back after he has lived with another woman, someone he has been seeing behind my back for more than a year?"

"Why did you cry when you found out, then?"

"Because I was hurt! I was angry! Divorcing him was the nicest thing I could think of to do! If you only knew some of the things I thought about doing."

Now Tara knew she had pushed her mother too far. She didn't want to hear this. She didn't want to be reminded of the screaming and the fighting, the shouts into the telephone about wanting to kill herself or him. She didn't want to think again of her mother's friends coming over to talk to her, to plead with her to not do anything foolish.

Could her mother really think Tara didn't know? Was it possible she thought that, once the kids were in bed, they heard none of the discussions, the arguing, the crying, the threats, the slammed doors, the cars racing away in the night? She wanted to tell her mother that she believed her mother still loved her dad and wanted him back. She was mad at him and he had been wrong, but she had cried because she was losing him.

The only problem was that her mother had heard all that before from Jeff. She was ready for it. "Whatever love I ever had for that man," she would say, "has long since been stomped in the dirt."

Tara didn't want to give her mother the chance to say that again. Not now. Not when Tara was about to leave for ten days. What she wanted right then was to go back a few minutes, back before she had raised the subject and got her mother even more upset. Part of her wanted to talk only of the pain of losing her father and seeing her mother so angry and hateful, because that was all that mattered to her. But another part of her wanted to put it aside, to push it back, to not have to think about it ever again.

She didn't want to go away, not now. But there was no turning back. Ray cried every night and hid it from Mom, and Jeff was angry. For some reason, she didn't know why, Tara felt as if she was the only hope of fixing the problem. She believed that if she talked long enough to her mother and got the chance to talk to her dad, she could make them see that this had all been a mistake.

Her father couldn't love some other woman more than he loved her mom. She could make him see that. She could remind him how much she loved him and how horrible it was at home without him. But if she wasn't there, what then? She knew she was considered just a child, and she even knew she bothered her mother by constantly talking about it.

But what else could she do? She felt as if she was hanging over the side of a cliff and that everyone else was just watching, even those who had caused her to slip over the edge. She was going to have to fix this all by herself. Was there something else she could have done, something she should have said or not said that would have kept her parents in love with each other?

She could have been a better daughter, she knew that. And while she didn't know what it was she had done or not done, she knew she wanted her parents back together so badly that she would make herself find out. Her mother had told her over and over that it was not her fault, and in a way she knew that was true. She couldn't imagine having done something that would make her father fall in love with somebody else.

But maybe if she had been more lovable and easier to talk to and more encouraging, her father would have wanted to spend every spare minute at home. She could have been the glue that kept her family together. She still could be. Except that she was being sent away.

"Now boarding all rows," the loudspeaker said.

She remained seated, but her mother stood and reached for her. Tara stood slowly, and her mother hugged her, speaking quickly in her ear. "You have a good time, and don't worry about us. We'll be fine. This is all for the best. Trust me."

Tara wanted to wrap her arms around her mother's neck and hold her so tightly that everything she wanted and needed to say would be understood. She wanted to squeeze so hard that her mother would know that she didn't want to go anywhere, that she wanted to stay and to be the perfect daughter so that everything could be put back the way it was.

But she couldn't make herself return her mother's hug. Her mother had said to trust her, and trusting anyone was something she might never do again. The person she wanted and needed to trust more than anyone else in the world didn't even live in her house anymore. And her mother, the one she also desperately wanted to trust, was sending her away at the wrong time.

If her parents were never going to get back together, if her family would never be the same, she hoped the plane would crash. She was in the middle of the surging crowd down the jetway when she turned to see if her mother was still watching and waving.

At first she didn't see her, but just before she turned back to get out of people's way, she caught a glimpse of her mother hurrying away, glancing at her watch.

If she thought she could have got away with it, Tara would have darted out of the airport and found her way to Suzanne's house. But it was too late for that. As she settled into her seat by the window, she buried her face in her hands and cried.

2

Aunt Bev

Tara had never flown alone before, and she was nervous, besides being heartbroken. The two-hour flight gave her a chance to calm down and compose herself. She was fascinated by the sky and the massive, fluffy clouds of pure white. It looked as if she could reach out and scoop up a handful. But when the plane dipped into them, the clouds appeared to thin out and disappear into a fog, causing the plane to bounce and jump.

Tara loved Aunt Bev, her mother's youngest sister. Even though her mother often complained that "Bev married beneath her class" and that she had "gotten religion," Aunt Bev was Tara's favorite. Sure, her other aunts and uncles, especially on her father's side, were wealthy and seemed to have been everywhere. But Aunt Bev was so special, so wonderful.

Aunt Bev's husband, Uncle Dale, was quiet but nice, and he seemed like such a good father. Her cousins Amy and Jennifer were fun because they idolized her. She smiled thinking about it. They would be sure to make her feel good. Even though she didn't want to be away from home when everything seemed to be falling apart, if she had to go somewhere, it was to Aunt Bev's that she'd rather go.

She had a lot in common with Amy and Jennifer's older brother Dallas too. He was a little less than a year older than she was, and he was all sports, through and through. He had never treated her like just a girl, and he had included her when he and his friends got together to play ball, no matter what those friends said or thought. Of course, after she showed she was nearly as good an athlete as Dallas and better than most of them, they grudgingly had to welcome her too. She looked forward to seeing Dallas's best friend, Jimmy. He was a funny kid, but shy and awkward around her.

The flight had been good for Tara, and she looked forward to being greeted at the airport. The agent had told her to tell someone if her aunt wasn't there as had been arranged. She chuckled at the thought. Aunt Bev was the most organized person she had ever met. In fact, when Tara thought of her she thought of neat rooms, piles of laundry perfectly folded, food in the oven, books being read to the girls, conversations with her son Dallas, and a big hug for her husband, Uncle Dale, when he came in hot and dirty from a day's work on the road.

That last memory made the lump rise again in Tara's throat. She had memories of her parents kissing when her dad got home from work. But how long ago was that? When was the last time she had seen them enjoy and appreciate and love each other? It had been almost a year since her mother had got an anonymous letter. Tara hadn't learned about it until months later when Jeff told her, but apparently her mother had been suspicious of her dad for a long time.

He seemed distracted, short tempered, and not affectionate toward his wife or any of the kids the way he once had been. He was gone earlier in the morning and home later at night. He took more business trips and was gone longer. Tara remembered her mother going through his desk, his papers, his bills. She remembered the day her mother sat in the middle of the floor, her hand full of receipts, her head down, weeping.

Then came the first fight, the accusation, the denial, the argument, the slammed door, the car racing away. After that came explanations, a new effort on Dad's part. He was home more, he took Mom out more. But the fights were more frequent, the cooling off periods longer. Soon he was gone even more.

It all swam in her head. Could it be true, she had wondered, that Mom was right? Had she grown old and ugly while a younger woman caught his eye? Tara had never thought of her mother as old and ugly. She showed some age as she reached her mid-thirties, and maybe her face seemed a little harder and colder than it had. But she was raising three children and was a busy, hardworking woman. She was still in shape, knew how to dress well, and looked great any time she went out. Anyway, what if she had fallen apart and become fat and ugly? Wasn't she still their mom and Dad's wife? Shouldn't he have loved her anyway?

She couldn't believe her dad would really love someone other than her mother. Dad was a handsome if small man, with dark hair and a great, toothy smile. Everybody loved him, especially women who thought he was cute and smooth, whatever that meant. He was five years older than Mom but looked a little younger than she did. Was it possible this new woman—the one people called his girl friend—was fifteen years younger than Mom? Why would Dad be interested in someone that young?

Tara didn't want to think about it anymore. She knew it would be almost impossible to keep her mind off it ever again, but she wanted to enjoy this time at the O'Neils, even if everything on the farm reminded her of how she wished her family could be.

She stopped in the tiny airplane washroom on her way out, just to make sure it didn't appear she had been crying. She splashed cold water on her face, brushed her hair vigorously, checked the collar on her light jacket, and stood straight before the mirror. She was ready.

On her way up the jetway, she saw Aunt Bev looking for her in the crowd. It was kind of fun to see without being seen, but she didn't want her aunt to worry that she had not made the flight. Aunt Bev. Never a fashion plate, she dressed for function rather than for looks, but she always looked great. Today she wore jeans, a sweater, and a light jacket that looked almost like Tara's. And she was alone. Her kids must still be in school for a few days.

As Tara emerged from the jetway, Aunt Bev saw her, smiled, and waved. Tara grinned and hurried toward her, noticing that her aunt's smile was forced and that she was working to keep her chin from quivering. Aunt Bev knew the whole story, of course, because such things tend to get around in a big family. Tara, who had nearly composed herself, embraced her aunt before they both burst into tears.

Beverly O'Neil was the type of aunt who knew what to do in difficult situations. She kept her head buried near Tara's shoulder while leading her to an empty lounge where they could both just sit and cry awhile. "We'll pick up Amy and Jennifer from school on the way home," she managed, "and Dallas will be home after practice, around six, in time for dinner."

Good, Tara thought. "What about Uncle Dale?"

"He gets home Monday from a job in Indiana," she said. "He's looking forward to seeing you."

Aunt Bev was so sweet. Ten years younger than Tara's mother, she was a cute woman with big eyes and wide open features, short hair almost as dark as her older sister's, but softer. She even had a few freckles, which made her look even younger. She wasn't what you would call skinny, but she seemed strong and outdoorsy while still looking very feminine. "This has to be very difficult for you," she said suddenly, holding Tara's hands in her own.

Tara nodded, fighting tears again.

"Oh, you poor, sweet dear," Aunt Bev said. And they embraced again.

"I hate it!" Tara whispered as her aunt held her close. "I just hate it! I want them back together!"

"I know," Aunt Bev said, stroking her hair. "I know. So do I. I'm praying."

"For them to get back together?"

"Some," she admitted. "Mostly I'm praying for you kids. I don't think your mom or dad want to work on the marriage."

Tara nodded miserably. "I'm OK now, if we have to get going."

Aunt Bev stood. "Yeah, we probably should. You're a strong, brave girl."

"You know what?" Tara said as they hurried out to the car. "I feel like I can be honest with you."

"Of course you can," her aunt said, turning to look at her.

"I'm not strong or brave."

Aunt Bev put her arm around Tara as they continued. "I know. I just meant right then, that you were able to pull yourself together and get on with what we have to do today. I know this all seems like a nightmare, and it is. But we have to work through it and not let it destroy us."

When they were in the car and Aunt Bev had paid for parking, Tara spoke again. "That's what it's doing to Mom, you know. Destroying her."

"Is it?" Aunt Bev said, and Tara was struck by the fact that she didn't know another living adult to whom she could talk like this. Anyone else would have immediately told her that she was wrong, that her mother was going to survive this and be stronger for it and that everything would work out for the best. A teacher had told her that a divorce is much better for kids than a bad marriage. *That* was a big help. Tara didn't want her parents to have a divorce *or* a bad marriage. She wanted things back the way they used to be.

"Clare has always been pretty high-strung," Aunt Bev said, and it was obvious to Tara that that was a nice way of saying that her aunt had never understood her mother. "But I love her to death," her aunt added. "I really do."

"Can you talk to her?" Tara asked.

"I've tried," Aunt Bev said. "But she thinks I'm too young to know anything. And anyway, I don't think she appreciates me too much." As soon as she had said that, Tara's aunt shook her head and apologized. "I shouldn't talk that way, Tara. You know your mom and I have had our differences over the years, but I certainly don't need to bring you into it. My priorities are not her priorities, and there's no way to prove that either of us is right or wrong."

Oh, yes there is, Tara thought, but she couldn't put a finger on why she thought so. It seemed to her that Uncle Dale and Aunt Bev saw a lot more value in people than in things. Though they lived in an old farmhouse on sparse acreage and didn't have new cars or a bathroom for every kid, their home sure seemed special. It was just like her aunt, too, to not want to say anything about anybody who wasn't there.

"I do think it's fair to say that your mother has given up on the marriage, though. I know she's told you that because she said so."

"She told you she talked to me about it?"

Aunt Bev nodded. "She said this is not going down so well with you. She says your brothers have accepted it but you haven't."

"My brothers have accepted it! Is that what she said, really?"

Aunt Bev nodded.

"I can't believe this! Ray cries himself to sleep every night, and half the time he wants to crawl in with Jeff. Jeff lets him, only if he'll promise not to tell that Jeff's sneaking out after midnight."

"Jeff's sneaking out?"

Tara nodded. "He meets his friends on the track team. I think they go drinking and partying."

"And your mother doesn't know?"

Tara shook her head. "I'm not going to squeal."

"You're going to feel bad if something happens to him, Tara."

"Like what?"

"What if he got hurt in an accident, and you knew he was out when he wasn't supposed to be?"

"I never thought of that. But still, I don't want to tell on him. What kind of a sister would that be? I know he's feeling as bad about this as I am, but he just handles it different."

"And that's why your mother thinks he's accepted it?"

"I guess."

Aunt Bev pulled into the parking lot of a small elementary school and looked at her watch. "That reminds me of Mom," Tara said. "She's always looking at her watch."

"You know why I look at my watch?" her aunt said. "Because I can hardly wait to see my sweeties."

Tara smiled, thinking how corny that sounded. She was sure Amy and Jennifer would cringe if they knew their mother had said that about them. But she wished with all her heart that her mother felt the same about her.

3

At the Farm

When the bell rang, elementary school kids bounded from the building. The boys wrestled and played four square; the girls jump roped and ran together. Amy and Jennifer O'Neil, however, ran straight for their mother's old station wagon.

"Tara! Tara!" they squealed, as she leaped from the car to hug them.

"Did you bring me anything?" first-grader Jennifer asked.

"No, Jen, sorry," Tara said. "I only had time to bring you me. Is that enough?"

Jennifer looked disappointed, but Amy said, "More than enough."

Jennifer stared at her older cousin as they all piled back into the car, and even though there was plenty of room, she insisted on sitting on Tara's lap. She looked deep into Tara's eyes.

"How does somebody get pretty like you?" she asked.

Tara laughed and squeezed her. "You're already prettier than me, Jenny!"

"Can we play with you when we get home?" fourth-grade Amy asked.

"No," their mother broke in. "Tara and I are going to be fixing dinner together, because we have a lot to talk about."

"Can we help?" the girls asked.

"C'mon, you never want to help," Aunt Bev said. "Why don't you just play outside until we're ready for you to help set the table."

"Oh," Amy said, "I know what you're going to talk about."

Tara looked sharply at her aunt, hoping it wasn't true that the little girls knew. Bev shook her head slightly.

Jennifer chimed in. "You're gonna talk about Uncle Fred and Aunt Clarice not lovin' each other anymore."

Tara sighed and dropped her head. Bev scolded Jennifer by simply shouting her name.

"I'm sorry," Jennifer said.

"I am too, Tara," her aunt said. "She didn't hear that from us. Maybe Dallas said something, or maybe she overheard some phone conversations. You know how hard it is to keep something like this from little ears. We—"

Tara stopped her with a forgiving wave. She understood, but she hated the sound of the truth. Her parents *didn't* love each other anymore, and everybody knew it. Suddenly little Jennifer didn't seem so cute, sitting there on her lap. Tara knew it wasn't Jenny's fault. The only problem was, she didn't know whose fault it was.

If her father was really in love with another woman, then it was *his* fault. If her mother was lying about him for some reason, it was *her* fault. Her brother said it was true and that he had seen the other woman with his dad. But he said it was his mother's fault because she had become so mean and hard to live with.

"Any man would want someone else if he had to live with Mom," Jeff had said. But that didn't sound right to Tara.

They rode in silence the rest of the way to the O'Neil farm. Tara felt clumsy not saying anything, but she was too upset to talk. Her world was coming to an end, and it was affecting everybody around her, her brothers, her cousins, her aunt. Why, oh why, couldn't everything be put back the way it was before? The families had shared such fun holidays and reunions. Now nothing would ever be the same.

Half an hour later Tara was peeling potatoes in the kitchen, idly watching the girls play outside near the barn. After waiting several minutes for her aunt to begin the conversation, Tara spoke.

"You know what my mother has been saying lately?"

"No, what?"

"She's been saying we all have to get serious."

"About what?"

"About everything. That's what she says, no matter what's going on. Jeff is only a second faster than he was last year in the four hundred meters, so Mom says he needs to get serious."

"Meaning?"

"Work harder, I guess. Get in better shape. Take better care of himself. I don't know."

"As I recall, he's pretty fast in the four hundred as it is."

"Oh, he is. But we all have to get serious about everything. Ray has to get serious about getting more customers on his route if he ever wants to be paper carrier of the year."

"Paper carrier of the year! I thought he was the youngest one in—"

"He is. That's just it. That isn't good enough. It's not enough to be the youngest. He has to be the best."

"But aren't there lots of high schoolers who still have paper routes?"

"Sure, and one of them usually wins the honor, because they can drive and do their routes quicker, even with a lot more customers."

"So, Tara, what does my sister want *you* to get serious about?"

"This."

"This?"

"This whole mess with her and Dad."

"I'd say you're pretty serious about it already." Aunt Bev dried her hands, grabbed another potato peeler, and joined Tara.

"She wants me to get serious about getting over it. Does she really think I'm gonna get over it? I'm not even going to accept it, let alone get over it."

Potatoes and meat were baking and vegetables were simmering when Aunt Bev and Tara went for a walk, passing the girls who called out, "Can you play with us later?"

"Later!" Tara yelled back.

She loved this farm in the spring. The air was crisp, the ground was soft and green. "If we walk around the corral," her aunt said, "we'll be out by the road when the Calabresis bring Dallas home."

Tara ran her fingers along the peeling paint of the fence. Aunt Bev asked if she had talked to her father yet.

"Not since he moved out. He was going to talk to us, the whole family, before he left, but Mom made such a fuss that he just left."

"What did he want to tell you?"

"I guess that he was in love with someone else," Tara said. "At least that's what Jeff says. I wouldn't believe it, even if Dad said it. It's a mistake, that's all. A terrible mistake. Maybe he couldn't help himself, or maybe Mom made him mad. But he didn't want to fall in love with someone else. Why would he? Why would he want to do that to Mom or to us? If I could just talk to him…"

"What would you say, Tara?"

Tara turned and leaned back against the corral. She crossed her feet at the ankles and shrugged. "I guess I'd just cry and plead with him to come home."

"Do you think that would do any good? Hasn't your mother tried that?"

"No! She's the one who kicked him out, remember. She begged him to tell her it wasn't true when she first accused him, but he was just quiet. Then she got mad. Now she's gotten serious."

"Following her own advice, huh?"

Tara nodded. "She's always been strong and tough, but I've never seen her like this. She has a lawyer, and she's doing everything she can to get back at Daddy. She wants as much of his money as she can get, alimony and child support and all that stuff."

Bev looked concerned. "How do you know all this?"

"Mom tells me. She says too many things were kept from her when she was a kid and that she decided to not keep her children in the dark."

"Maybe so, but she's going to turn you against him and—" Aunt Bev stopped in mid-sentence. "There I go again," she said. "You must forgive me when I do that, judging my sister without knowing both sides."

"Oh, don't worry about it, Aunt Bev. Mother doesn't even pretend she's not trying to turn us against Daddy. She says horrible things about him all the time. The other day she said something about having her lawyer get some paper so he wouldn't be able to see us again."

Aunt Bev didn't respond. She just looked worried and concerned.

Tara continued. "If my mother did that, I'd run away from home."

"Oh, honey, no."

"I would! Nobody can keep me from my dad. How would I ever be able to get him back if I couldn't see him or talk to him?"

Still Aunt Bev said nothing. She just opened her arms and held Tara and let her cry again.

After a minute, Tara chuckled through her tears. "I don't want to look like a big baby when Dallas gets home." She wiped her eyes on her jacket sleeves, knowing her face was red and puffy.

From over the hill Tara heard the hiss of tires. "That's the Calabresis' new van," her aunt said.

"That's not all they have new, is it?" Tara said. "Dallas wrote me something about a horse, a horse with a funny name."

"Star Diamond," Aunt Bev said.

"Yeah. It's Jimmy's?"

"Uh-huh."

"Will he be in the van?"

"The horse or Jimmy?"

Tara laughed. "Jimmy."

"Should be. He and Dallas are on the soccer team at school."

"At school? I thought the soccer team was their own."

"They have their own too, but that's in a different league. The school finally started a sports program, and the Baker Street Sports Club guys are on all the teams."

The van rolled to a stop, and Dallas clambered out, shoes in one hand, bag in the other. "Hey, Tara!" he said. "How ya doin'?"

Tara smiled shyly and couldn't keep from laughing when she saw Jimmy peeking out at her. "Hi, Jim!" she said, waving with her fingers.

He muttered a greeting and slumped back into his seat. Dallas had told her before that Jimmy thought she was great, but Jimmy would never admit it.

"I hear you've got a new horse!" she said.

Jimmy turned back to her. "Yeah."

"Maybe I can come over and see him sometime while I'm here."

"OK."

"You don't sound too excited about that."

"I am. You can come. Tonight?"

"Well, maybe tomorrow."

As the van pulled away, Dallas smiled. "He's got it bad for you, Tara."

"Oh, he does not, Dallas. Now quit it."

Dallas punched her playfully on the shoulder, and she pretended to come after him as he skipped away. They laughed as if they were little kids again. Tara felt as if she was at the farm for the first time as a four-year-old, playing hide-and-seek in the fields and running through the meadows. For an instant she almost forgot how sad she was.

Almost.

4

Getting Serious

That night at dinner, Tara realized that she had heard her aunt pray for the first time. Uncle Dale had always been around when she visited before, and he had always prayed before they ate. She liked his prayers because they were always different, and it seemed as if he meant every word. At her house, they said a rhyming verse about the food on Sunday afternoons, but most of the time they just dug in.

Aunt Bev had prayed, "Lord, thank you that Tara can be with us, even though it's under difficult circumstances. Show her Your love, and please let us be instruments for Your love to flow through to her. We know that the most important thing is that she and her brothers and her parents come to You, because You are the only one who can miraculously heal broken marriages."

The rest of the prayer was for the food, and for Uncle Dale while he worked, but Tara's mind stayed on that part about God being the one who could heal broken marriages. Tara's hope was in being able to talk to her dad. She believed with all her heart that she could convince him to come back to her mother. But she wouldn't mind God's help. Maybe she would pray about that herself.

Tara wasn't used to praying, except for Sunday dinner. At her church the pastor prayed, and he used big, religious sounding words she didn't understand. She believed in God, because her family had always gone to church, but they never talked about it.

At times she wished she knew more about God. Sometimes, sitting in church during a long prayer or a choir performance, she would study the stained glass windows or some of the paintings and wonder about God. Who was He? Where was He? He seemed all right to her, but He was pretty easy to forget about when she wasn't in church. And church was only Sunday mornings.

When she was at the O'Neil's, God seemed different. There was something friendlier, more familiar about Him here. The O'Neils seemed to know more about Him, expect more from Him, care more about Him even on days other than Sunday.

That had always interested her, but it had also made the O'Neils seem very religious to her. She had never heard any of them swear like she and her brothers and especially her parents often did. She guessed that was why her mother had said that Aunt Bev had "gotten religion." Her mother said, "I remember when Beverly could drink me under the table. Now she won't even serve champagne on a special occasion."

"Yeah," her father had said, "and I get the clear message that if I'm gonna smoke at the farm, it's gonna be outside. They don't even have ashtrays."

"That has nothing to do with her religion," Tara's mother had told him. "Nonsmokers just don't want the smell in their homes."

"Well, I happen to like the smell," her dad said. Tara wondered if that could be true.

For all the differences, big and small, between the families, Tara loved the O'Neils. She felt special when she was there, and she liked the way they treated each other. The kids fought like all kids do, but they didn't scream at each other and say things they would have to take back later. Uncle Dale and Aunt Bev acted like they were still in love. Tara would see them holding hands while they walked in the meadow or in the field. Once, while they were all watching an old movie on television, Aunt Bev actually sat on his lap, right in front of everybody!

Her aunt and uncle caught her watching them, giggled, and then kissed. Uncle Dale winked at Tara and smiled.

And Dallas. He was the nicest kid her age she had ever met, cousin or not. He didn't seem embarrassed when it was his turn to read the Bible or pray during their family Bible time after dinner each night. She would have been able to tell if he was just faking it and made fun of it later. But he didn't. This religious thing was as important to him as it was to his parents. Only he told her once that religion had nothing to do with it.

"Well, it sure seems religious," she said. "All that Bible stuff and praying. If that's not religion, I don't know what it is."

"It's Jesus," he had said, and he was so matter-of-fact that she could hardly believe it. "It's not some ritual or churchy thing. We believe in Jesus, and we're not ashamed of it."

"Well, we believe in Jesus, too," she had said. "But we don't talk about it all the time."

He had asked her what she meant when she said her family believed in Jesus, and she had said, "Well, what do *you* mean?"

He tried to explain it to her, but she had been too young to understand, and she quickly changed the subject. Now it was interesting to her that the O'Neils were the same as always. After the dishes were done and the younger girls went to bed, Tara sat in the living room talking with Dallas and her aunt.

"This is going to drive me crazy," she said. "I love you all, but I feel trapped having to be here when I should be home trying to talk to my dad."

"Does your dad want to talk to you?" Aunt Bev asked.

"I don't know. Why wouldn't he?"

"Maybe he's embarrassed. Maybe he knows you wouldn't approve of what he's doing."

Tara flinched. "Do *you* think he's doing what Mom thinks he's doing? Living with another woman, I mean?"

Aunt Bev didn't say anything. Tara could tell by the look on her face that that was exactly what she thought. Why did everyone believe her mother? How did she know? Had Dad confessed? What did he say about it?

"My brother claims he has Dad's new phone number. I'd like to talk to him."

"To your dad or your brother?" Dallas said.

"Both," Tara said. "Don't get me wrong. I like bein' here, and I like you guys a lot. But I'm going crazy not being able to do anything about my mom and dad."

"How about we try to get your mind off it for a while?" her aunt said. "Want to play some games?"

Tara shrugged. "Not really."

"Honey, there's really nothing you can do. We'll just keep praying for them and see what God does."

"You think God knows what's going on?"

"Sure," Dallas said. "He knows everything. He made them. He cares about them. He wants them to come to Him."

Tara scowled. "Come to Him? You mean He wants them to pray to Him about it?"

Aunt Bev started to say something, but Dallas broke in. "Well, yeah, He wants them to pray about it, but mostly He wants them to become Christians."

"We *are* Christians!" she shot back, almost offended. "You know that!"

"Well," Dallas said, "I'm talking about people who receive Christ."

Tara squinted. She had no idea what he was talking about. "We go to church," she said, "and we hear about God and Jesus, and they pray there, and we pray for Sunday dinner at home. We're Christians."

"Does your dad believe in Christ?" Dallas pressed.

"Dallas," his mother cautioned him.

"It's all right," Tara said to her aunt. Yes, my father is a Christian too. I mean, he hasn't been to church the last few weeks because he hasn't been living with us, but he's a Christian just like the rest of us."

"What I'm getting at—" Dallas began, but his mother cut him off.

"Dallas, I think this is something we can discuss with Tara tomorrow. I promised her she could call her mother and her best friend tonight, and I think now would be a good time."

"But, Mom, Tara says her dad is a Christian, and yet he leaves his family for another woman."

"Dallas, we don't know all the facts," his mother said. "Let's let Tara make her phone calls, and maybe all of us can talk about this again sometime."

Tara went upstairs to get ready for bed and use the extension phone in the guest bedroom, but she had forgotten the piece of paper with the instructions on how to dial the telephone credit card number so her aunt and uncle wouldn't have to pay for the calls. When she slipped back downstairs to get it, she overheard Dallas and his mother in the kitchen.

"I still don't see how they can call themselves Christians, Mom. She had no more idea what I was talking about than the man in the moon."

That's for sure, Tara thought.

"I know, honey," Aunt Bev was saying, "and it was admirable for you to try to explain it. But she's very upset, and her mother is not happy about what she thinks is the overemphasis on religion in this house. You and I know it's not religion, and there's nothing I'd like better than to see Tara—in fact, that whole family—come to Christ, but we're going to have to move cautiously. If my sister thought we were trying to push Tara to our way of thinking about Jesus the first night she's here, Clarice would be furious. She might even make Tara come home."

Home! Tara thought. *As much as I love these people, home is where I want to be! Maybe I should tell my mother that they were trying to preach to me. She'd send for me right now!*

Tara crept back upstairs with her credit card number, thinking about the phrase she had heard again: "come to Christ." What *were* they talking about? Why did this all have to be so complicated?

She called Suzanne Yorty first. "Hey, Suz," she said, and Suzanne squealed.

"Tara, how are ya?"

"I'm OK, but I wish I was home, you know what I mean?"

Tara told Suzanne about her day, from leaving the airport to sitting in the O'Neils' living room.

"Oh, wow," Suzanne said. "Don't worry, you're a Christian. You guys go to church and everything. If they want somebody to work on, they ought to try my family. We haven't been to church in years. They ought to go after somebody who needs it."

Suzanne told Tara that the talk around the community was that all the rumors about her father were true. Tara's father lived with his new girl friend in an apartment in the city, and they planned to be married as soon as his divorce was final.

"Where did you hear that?" Tara demanded.

"It's all over the place," Suzanne said.

"Come on, tell me."

"OK, I heard it from my mom, but Tara, you can't say anything."

"How does she know?"

"She hears things. What do you think? C'mon, Tar', you're not still pretending this isn't happening, are you?"

"I'm trying. Hoping. Praying."

"Uh-oh."

"Don't worry. But listen, Suz, you gotta do something for me. I'm gonna call my mom in a little while, but if I talk to Jeff, she'll be right there and know what I'm doing. So do me a favor, OK?"

"If it means talking to Jeff, of course."

"It does. He says he's got my dad's new phone number, and I want it."

"What are you gonna do with it, Tara?"

"What do you think?"

"You think that's smart?"

Tara sighed. "Suz," she said, "I don't know anything anymore, except that if my dad won't talk to me, *I'll* talk to *him*. Say you'll do it. I'll call you tomorrow night for the number."

"Of course I'll do it. What are friends for?"

When Tara talked to her mother, she said nothing about what she and Dallas and Aunt Bev had talked about. Her mother seemed distracted anyway and said she would call Tara in a few days. *Clearly,* Tara thought, *she doesn't want to be bothered with me. That's why I'm here.*

5
The Sky

Tara didn't sleep. All she could think of was trying to get a chance to talk to her father. She had agreed to call Suzanne at three the next afternoon to get her father's new phone number. But what was she going to say to him? Could she convince him without facing him, without letting him see her tears? What if she couldn't?

In the morning she went to Jimmy Calabresi's with Dallas and got to ride the beautiful palomino, Star Diamond. He was a powerful, almost frightening force beneath her, but she could tell he was gentle by nature, and he responded well to her commands and urgings. Jimmy had taught him to react to the reins. Tara fed Star Diamond a carrot and a sugar cube, and he nuzzled her.

Jimmy, dark-haired and pudgy, led the horse back to its stable where he wrestled off the saddle and brushed down Star Diamond. He pointed the stallion toward the corral and slapped him on the rear. The horse galloped off, snorting and sniffing the air.

"Are we gonna do the usual today," Jimmy asked, "even with her here?"

"Don't let me get in the way of whatever you usually do," Tara said. "I can walk back to the farm, or—"

"Oh, it's not that," Jimmy said. "It's just that we wouldn't want you to be uncomfortable."

"Why would I feel uncomfortable?" Tara said. "I can do anything guys can do, and you know it."

Jimmy laughed and shook his head. "Do I ever! You can outrun me, outthrow me, and hit almost as far as I can."

"Farther," Tara said, but she was teasing. She had seen Jimmy hit some balls into the creek behind Mrs. Ferguson's place, where the Baker Street Sports Club played baseball. She had hit a home run on that field too, but it had been a line drive that skipped past the center fielder.

Dallas was strangely silent.

Jimmy said, "Well, what we do is we jog out past the pasture and up over that ridge." He pointed in the distance.

"I can jog that far. In fact, I can probably get there before you."

"I'm not talking about a race," Jimmy said. "I can't run that far very fast, but it helps get me in shape to jog it."

"So, what do you do when you get there?" Tara asked.

"That's the part you might not be comfortable with," Jimmy said.

Tara smiled and shook her head. "What are you guys up to, something dirty?"

Jimmy laughed. "The opposite," he said. "We lie on our backs, just over the crest of the hill where the meadow starts. We're surrounded by tiny yellow flowers, the ground is cool on our backs, the sun is in our eyes, and we stare at the sky."

"That sounds awful," Tara teased. "It sounds more like something girls would do than boys, so maybe you're the one who would be uncomfortable with me around."

Jimmy shook his head. "It's what we do then," he said.

"I can hardly wait to hear this," Tara said. "But let me tell you now, if you can do it, I can do it."

"But you might not want to," Jimmy said. "We read this." He reached behind some rusted tools on an old wood shelf and produced a dog-eared, grimy paperback copy of a modern translation of the Bible.

Tara tried not to show her disappointment. That was the same thing the O'Neils had done the night before with Amy slowly reading a chapter. It was all right, but Tara hadn't got much out of it.

She shrugged. "I don't mind," she said, but it sure seemed like a bore. "You're into this stuff too?" she asked Jimmy.

He smiled shyly. "Yeah. I go to church with Dallas all the time now. I'm a Christian."

Tara wanted to ask, "Who *isn't*?" but she just said, "Me too."

Jimmy's reaction was almost embarrassing. "Really? I didn't know that! When did it happen?"

When did it happen? Tara repeated in her mind. *What's with these people? Nothing happened!*

She decided to take the spotlight off herself. "Well, when did it happen to *you*?"

"Almost a year ago," Jimmy said.

"And how about you, Dallas?"

"When I was six."

Tara noticed Dallas ever so faintly signaling Jimmy to get off the subject. Though Tara assured both boys that she had no problem with jogging with them and even reading the Bible with them, she racked her brain to make all this make sense. What was it that happened to Jimmy and to Dallas at a certain time that made them more religious, or whatever?

"So, you coming with us or not?" Jimmy asked.

"Let's go."

Jimmy jogged out of the corral and down along the road, with Dallas loping easily behind. Tara would have raced to the lead if she had known exactly where they were going. Within a quarter mile or so, Jimmy was panting. Obviously, he was going faster than usual to impress Tara. But she wasn't impressed, because she would have already been to wherever it was they were going if she didn't have to slow down for him.

As Jimmy's pace slackened, Dallas slipped past Tara and took the Bible from him, then strode out ahead. Tara stayed with him as Jimmy struggled to keep up. Now *this* she liked. Dallas had long, powerful, smooth strides, and she settled into his pace. Jimmy pounded along behind, gasping for breath, his steps labored and heavy.

Jimmy fell back as Dallas turned a corner and charged up an incline. Tara envied Dallas's strength, but by digging in and pushing herself, she was able to keep up. She could hear him breathing deeply and knew that because she was lighter, she had as much endurance, though not the same strength.

When Dallas reached the crest of the hill, he stopped abruptly, and she had to skip to avoid crashing into him. They both laughed, trying to catch their breath, their hands on their hips.

Jimmy walked slowly up the hill. "Usually I can make it running all the way," he managed. "But we don't usually go this fast."

The three of them stood in the bright morning sun, sweat trickling down their faces and making them shiver. Dallas gingerly led the way about ten feet down the other side of the grassy, flowery hill and stretched out on his back. Tara sat several feet away, her feet flat on the ground, her hands behind her for support. Jimmy flopped onto his side, still gasping. Tara turned her chin toward the sky and let the sun warm her face.

What a beautiful, beautiful day, she thought. *The sky, no clouds, the grass, all these flowers, and that grove of trees below.* She was nearly overcome with the beauty of it, and she realized that they were at a place where she could neither hear nor see any road or cars, and she couldn't see any telephone wires or anything man-made.

"We like this place," Dallas said, "because it looks like it must have looked when God created it."

Tara didn't say anything. She had been thinking almost the same thing. What perfect, unspoiled beauty!

"Stretch out on your back," Dallas said. "With the sun still low in the sky, you can look over there, and all you can see is blue. Even in your side vision, there's nothing but the blue sky. Man!"

Jimmy rolled onto his back. Tara carefully pushed with her hands and slid her feet down. It was true. Suddenly, as if a burst of blue had exploded on her brain, she saw nothing but seamless sky. Her complete field of vision was filled with one, solid, single, brilliant color.

It nearly made her dizzy. She felt the ground beneath her, and it was almost as if she could feel the earth spinning in space. The earth, the sky, the universe seemed so immense that Tara felt like a speck, an insignificant fraction of the whole. She wanted to say something, to express herself, to tell Dallas that she wondered how this must look at night. But for some reason he and Jimmy seemed small and unimportant, too.

The clear, blue sky overwhelmed her and left her speechless. It no longer seemed far away, and she knew she would never look at the sky the same way again. The blue seemed to begin at the end of her nose and extend for eternity. She tried to focus far away and imagine that she could see stars or planes or anything in the distance. But nothing was there. Only space so empty and so alive with color that it must not be vapor. It must be a solid. She was tempted to reach out and touch it, and that reminded her of how she had felt about the clouds while on the plane the day before.

The more Tara let the beauty of the sky work on her, the smaller she felt. There was something magnificent, mighty, powerful, majestic about the sky, in fact about the whole creation. She had been a city girl all her life, rich with things and money and opportunity, yet she had never lain in a meadow of flowers and gazed at the sky till it filled her senses.

She was envious of Dallas and Jimmy, and she hoped they never took this beauty for granted. She wanted to say so, but she didn't want to ruin the moment. Emotions washed over her that she didn't understand. For some reason she felt wrong, bad, guilty somehow. In spite of the beauty, of the breathtaking brilliance, she felt worse than small. She felt like an intruder, as if she didn't belong in this place.

Who was she to be here—and not just here in the country, but anywhere? Who was she to think her problems were of any importance to anyone? And wasn't she the one who had caused them in the first place? Wasn't there something she should have said or done or not said or not done that would have kept her parents together?

The place, the universe, space, creation was too big, too massive, too overpowering for her. While she couldn't tear her eyes away from the scene, she tried closing them for an instant, but the sky had been so bright and luminescent that even her shut eyes couldn't hold back the blue.

Part of her wanted to stay and be carried away by the beauty of the sky. She didn't ever want to look at anything else again. But another part of her wanted to turn away, to roll over, to leap to her feet, to run from it. She wanted to be away from anyone and everyone, to get back to somewhere safe. But where was that?

Her aunt's farmhouse with its cozy bed and fluffy quilts? That wasn't home. But home was a place of sadness and despair and anger. There was nowhere to go, no one to run to. Her mother had her own problems. Her father hadn't even called.

Tara's chest was heavy, her eyes wet with tears. Was she crying because of the beauty of this place or because of the pain and shame? She didn't know. All she knew was that she wanted to keep Jimmy and Dallas from knowing she was weeping. But she didn't want to reach up and brush her tears away because that would have blocked her view. That would have reminded her that she had a body, that she was anchored to the earth, that there were people around, and that she would not be able to forever lose herself in this scene.

But what was that noise? Paper rustling, pages turning. She didn't want to turn and look. One of the boys, probably Dallas, had opened that Bible. She would not look at him. She would look at nothing but the sky. For as terrifying and humbling as it was, it was her only escape right now. It was the only distraction from the knowledge that the real world still existed.

Tara knew she would rather be swallowed up by this shocking beauty than to face the real world with its hard truth. She tried to relax. She knew that if she breathed more deeply, she could make her heart beat more slowly. She could stop the flow of tears.

6
The Phone Call

When Dallas began to read, Tara wondered if he was praying.

"O Lord our God, the majesty and glory of your name fills all the earth and overflows the heavens. You have taught the little children to praise you perfectly."

If anything, the blue sky seemed bluer for the beauty of those words. Tara felt warm all over and knew she could talk to Dallas without spoiling the moment. "Where was that from?" she asked.

"Psalm eight, one and two," he said. "You like it?"

"Beautiful," she said dreamily.

"When we come out here tonight, I'll read the rest of the chapter by flashlight. You won't believe it."

She rolled onto her side and looked up at him, several feet away. "We're coming back here tonight?"

"Yeah," Jimmy interrupted. "If you think this is gorgeous in the daytime, you should see it at night."

Tara's heart raced. "That's just what I've been thinking! Honest! That very thing went through my mind."

She turned back to gaze at the sky. And Dallas read more. "O Lord, I will praise you with all my heart, and tell everyone about the marvelous things you do. I will be glad, yes, filled with joy because of you. I will sing your praises, O Lord God above all gods."

"What was that from?" she asked.

"First two verses of the next chapter," Dallas said.

Tara was struck that she had never heard a kid say or even read something like that before, yet it didn't sound stupid coming from Dallas. It sounded as if he meant it and wasn't embarrassed to say so.

"You like to read that?" she asked.

"I do," he said. "When I first came out here and saw that you could look at sky and only sky and could feel the presence of God, I didn't know how to say it. My dad told me it had already been said and that I should look in the psalms for beautiful ways of saying what I feel about God and what He has made."

"Don't kids make fun of you?" Tara said.

"Sometimes. Of course, I don't go around quoting Psalms all the time, you know."

"Yeah, but they must know you're like this."

Dallas chuckled. "Like this? Like what?"

"Like, you know, religious or whatever you call it."

"Yeah," Jimmy broke in. "They know. And yeah, they make fun of him sometimes. I know *I* did."

"But you don't now?"

"I'd be making fun of myself," Jimmy said. "I told you, I've become a Christian too."

"What were you before? Jewish?"

"No, I thought I was a Christian because I wasn't anything else. My grandparents used to take me to church when I visited them, so I figured I was whatever they were."

"What changed your mind?"

"O'Neil."

"How did he change your mind? What did he say?"

"It wasn't anything he said. Well, it sort of was. He was always reading his Bible and praying, and it seemed so weird that I tried to shame him out of it. He wouldn't play ball or go anywhere or do anything until he'd done his devotions."

"Devotions?"

"Yeah, reading and praying."

"Sounds like something a priest would do," Tara said.

Dallas laughed. "Do I look like a priest to you?"

"No, but I do wonder why you do it. I mean, devotions don't sound like something a kid would be interested in."

The three of them were sitting up now, pulling their jackets up around their shoulders.

"Let me tell you why I do it," Dallas said, and Tara was glad she didn't have to ask. She didn't want to appear too interested, but she really was. In fact, she was almost as curious about this as anything she had ever wondered about.

"Devotions are something you have when you're devoted to something or someone. I'm devoted to Christ, so I have devotions. It's not strange or weird or anything, and you don't have to live in a monastery to do it."

Tara nodded as if she understood. She didn't. Oh, she knew what the word meant. What she didn't know was how somebody could be that devoted to Christ. Sundays had always been enough religion for her. She believed God created the world and that He helped you out when you really needed it. But right now He wasn't doing anything for her. She needed Him more than ever, and she wanted a miracle. But she didn't really even know how to pray.

"You ought to tell her," Jimmy said, "why you're so devoted that you have devotions and that you've got me havin' 'em now too."

Tara was amazed at how these guys seemed to read her mind. Maybe she wasn't hiding too well the fact that she was still really puzzled.

"Tara," Dallas said slowly, "I want to tell you all about this, but I don't want to make you feel bad or get you in trouble, or even talk to you in front of Jimmy if you'd rather talk in private."

Tara *was* embarrassed, but not because Jimmy was there. She sensed that the mystery of the big difference between her family and Dallas's family was about to be revealed, and it scared her a little. Did Dallas really know how confused she was about this "coming to Christ" stuff? Could he know how it bothered her when he seemed to say that she and her family were not even Christians? Was there something she had been missing, or were Dallas and his family just more religious than hers?

"I don't mind talking about this in front of Jimmy," she said. "I mean, if something happened to him that hasn't happened to me, I wouldn't mind at least knowing about it. As long as you don't make me pray or do anything."

Dallas smiled. "I wouldn't do that, Tara. But I think I do know why this all seems so strange to you."

"You do? Why?"

"I just don't think you understand it the way God wants us to understand it."

"Now you sound like a preacher."

"Sorry. I don't mean to. You know I'm no great student or anything. This had to be explained to me too."

"Who explained it to you?"

"My parents."

"How did they know what it was all about?"

"Somebody told them. Then they studied for themselves in lots of Christian books, but especially the Bible. You know my dad has his devotions in the barn every morning, reading his Bible and praying before going to work."

"Even in the winter!" Jimmy said. "Dallas saw him out there one day in the freezing cold."

"That barn's not heated, is it?" Tara asked.

"Nope," Dallas said. "He was out there in his big, old easy chair, the one I thought he had thrown out years ago, and he was wrapped in a big quilt, reading under one bare light bulb."

"Reading his Bible?" Tara asked.

"Yup. And praying. He has this long prayer list of friends and relatives he prays for. I saw it once, and I was at the top of the list. That really got to me."

"You think my mom and dad are on that list?"

"Sure. And I'll bet you are too. He prays for everybody on both sides of the family."

Tara stood to stretch and moved closer to Dallas and Jimmy, now sitting on a rock. "And he does this, why? Because he's devoted to God like you are?"

"I wish I was as devoted as he is," Dallas says. "I admit I started having devotions because he was doing it."

"Do you ever miss?"

"Not very often, but sometimes I sleep in and then I want to get started having fun or doing something else and I don't want to have devotions."

"But he has them anyway," Jim said.

"Not always," Dallas admitted. "But I always wish I did."

"Why?"

"Because I believe God likes to hear from me."

Tara raised her eyebrows and scowled. "You're sounding a little crazy now, Dallas. Sorry."

Dallas shrugged. "Maybe there's a difference in what people think about God."

"There sure is," she said. "If I told anyone in my family or any of my friends that I prayed or read the Bible, they'd think I'd lost my mind. And if I told them I did it because God wanted to hear from me, they'd *know* I lost my mind."

Dallas rubbed his forehead and appeared to be thinking. "But if you were really devoted to Christ, you'd *want* to talk to Him, wouldn't you?"

"You mean pray? Yeah, I guess."

"I mean more than just when you're in trouble or want something. I think God wants us to know Him, and to know Him we have to talk to Him and read about Him."

Tara nodded slightly. "That sounds a little less crazy, but it's still strange, you have to admit."

"Maybe," Dallas said. "But I think it makes sense."

"I do too," Jimmy said, "but it didn't at first. Just like you, I just thought this whole thing was real religious."

"It *is*," Tara said. "You can't deny that!"

"Well, it sort of isn't," Jimmy said.

"I know," she said, "now you're gonna start in with that it's-not-a-religion-it's-a-person bit."

Jimmy smiled and nodded.

Dallas seemed to change the subject. "Tara," he said, "do you believe God created the world?"

"Of course."

"Did He make you?"

"In a way."

"In what way?"

"Well, He made man, and I'm part of mankind."

"Does it make sense that He would care about you personally?"

"I guess."

"If you were God, wouldn't you want to have the people you created know you? Talk to you? Learn about you? Like you?"

Tara thought about that. The way Dallas was saying it, he wasn't just trying to win an argument. She didn't feel trapped, but she wanted to be sure to not say the wrong thing. She wanted to answer honestly, and she knew if she did, she would open herself to the possibility that the God who created her wanted to know her and have her know Him.

That was almost too good to be true. But it did make sense. "Yes," she said carefully. "That makes sense."

"I have good news for you, Tara," Dallas said. "God is interested in you. In fact, He's devoted to you."

She laughed. "So He has devotions for me?"

Dallas smiled. "It wouldn't surprise me. The Bible says He loved us before we loved Him."

"What do you think God wants from me?" Tara asked.

Dallas shook his head. "What a question!"

Tara was offended. "Well, excuse me for not knowing what to ask! Just because I'm not some religious know-it-all—"

Dallas interrupted. "Tara, please! You know I wouldn't make fun of a question. I was serious. That was a great question. Not enough people know or even care what God might want from them. But there is an answer. He doesn't want much because we don't have much to offer. He only wants us. All of us."

"All of us? You mean everybody."

"That too, but I meant all of each of us."

"That *is* a lot," Tara said.

"Oh, I don't know," Dallas said. "Compared to Him, we really don't have much to offer, do we?"

Tara thought about that and about the gigantic sky that had filled her senses. "No, we sure don't," she said. "We sure don't."

A bell rang from Jimmy's back door, and he scrambled over the top of the ridge, hollering, "Yo! Mom! Up here!" He could see her, but he couldn't hear her from there. He skipped down the side of the hill, then ran back up.

"Phone call!" he said. "Phone for Tara!"

"For me?" Tara said, leaping to her feet. "We've got to get back. Ask her who it is." The three of them jogged down the hill to where they could hear.

"Ma! Who is it?"

"Her father! He called O'Neils, and Bev asked him to call here. He says he can't hold."

"Get his number!" Tara screamed.

7
The Difference

Tara stood panting in the Calabresis' kitchen, her face flushed, beads of perspiration tracing lines past each ear.

"I'm sorry, honey," Jimmy's mother said. "Your father was on his way to some meeting or another and just couldn't hold. I didn't think to ask for his number because I assumed you knew it, and by the time I heard that you wanted it, he had hung up."

Tara fought tears of frustration and anger, which Mrs. Calabresi misunderstood. "I'm sorry, dear," she said again. "I just didn't know—"

"It's not your fault," Tara said, trying to hide the quivering of her voice. "He just—" But she didn't finish. She wanted to spit out the words. Her dad didn't care enough to wait for her, didn't want her to call him, didn't want to face her questions, not even on the phone.

She was tempted to ask to use the phone anyway, to not wait for Suzanne to coax her dad's new number from Jeff. She wanted to just call Jeff directly and demand the number, then call her dad right away. She would tell him she knew he was there, that he should have waited for her. She would ask him how he could go so long without talking to her, what he was up to, what he was going to do about their family, and whether he loved them anymore.

But she couldn't do any of that. She didn't know whether Mrs. Calabresi knew anything that was going on. Since Jimmy's mother had not asked for her father's phone number, maybe she knew nothing and assumed he was calling from home or from his office. Tara hoped so. It was too embarrassing to have people know, to have them wonder and feel sorry for her. She knew kids whose parents were either separated or divorced, and it was something people just didn't talk about.

The last thing Tara wanted was for everybody to think about that every time she was around, for them to feel sorry for her and wonder about her. Worst of all, she didn't want people wondering what had gone wrong, what was the problem with a family whose parents didn't love each other anymore.

Both her mom and dad were acting that way lately, like they didn't care about the kids or the marriage. Tara just couldn't make herself believe it was true. She was convinced that down deep they still loved each other. Maybe they had got off the track somehow because they were too busy or too tired, or maybe the kids—she and her brothers—had been too much work for them.

Whatever it was, she believed, could be fixed, smoothed over, forgotten. She would give anything she had or would ever have to put it all back together again. But when her dad pulled something like this, when he made one small attempt to call and hung up at the first opportunity before talking to her, she began to ache. It was at times like this that she feared that the people were right who believed that her parents' marriage was over.

But if the marriage was over, the family as she knew it was over, and she would just as soon wish her own life was over.

Jimmy and Dallas seemed to sense how upset she was, so for the rest of the morning and early afternoon they didn't talk about her family or what they had talked about in the meadow.

They walked back to Dallas's place, and Aunt Bev packed them lunches to eat in the woods out behind the lower forty acres.

Tara enjoyed that, eating with her friends in the woods, but her mind was far away. She looked forward to talking with Suzanne at three o'clock. Strangely, she also looked forward to going back to the meadow after dark. That seemed an inviting, wonderful thing to her, and she didn't know why.

Part of it, she knew, was the excitement of being allowed to be out after dark, of being trusted to enjoy a half hour or an hour with her cousin and his friend without being suspected of getting into mischief. She also looked forward to how that big, pale blue sky would look when there was no sun and the stars would be set against the blackness of the night. She hoped against hope it wouldn't be cloudy. There would be nothing to see if the moon and stars were hidden.

It might be fun to be out there under an umbrella, shivering against a cold rain, but there sure wouldn't be much to look at.

Tara, Dallas, and Jimmy strolled lazily back from the woods across the furrows of the empty lower forty and reached the back porch at about two o'clock. To Tara's disappointment, clouds had formed and covered half the sky. Dallas noticed her scanning the horizon.

'That's not unusual around here for this time of the day," he said. "It'll clear up by tonight when we go back to the meadow."

"We're for sure going to do that?" Tara asked. "I mean, it's all right with your mother?"

"Already talked to her about it," he said. "We have to be home by nine-thirty and go straight to bed, but yeah, it's OK."

Tara knew she would be even more excited if she wasn't anxious about her dad, but she couldn't help that. At two-thirty she couldn't stand waiting any longer and asked her aunt if she could use the phone. When she reached Suzanne's number, however, Suzanne's mother told her that her best friend wasn't there.

"She's at your house, I think," Mrs. Yorty said. "She said she wanted to talk to your brother about something."

"OK," Tara said. "I'll try again at three."

"Well, I could have her call you there as soon as she gets back, hon."

"It's long distance."

"Oh, that's all right. I'll have her call you."

"Well, I'll try at three, and if she's still not back, you can have her call me."

Tara could tell from the sound of Mrs. Yorty's voice that she thought Tara was being a little strange. And she was, but she couldn't help it. She wanted that phone number worse than ever, and if she sounded a little frantic or a little foolish, that was too bad.

When she went back outside, Jimmy and Dallas were shooting baskets. Tara sat on the back porch steps, her chin in her hands, watching.

Dallas bounced a pass to her. "Wanna shoot with us?" he asked.

She fired the ball back to him and shook her head. "Nah. I'll just watch."

Jimmy began showing off, trying to make long shots that would have been half the length of a basketball court. He made about one in six, and Tara clapped and smiled. He pretended not to notice but kept firing away. The only problem was that, when he missed, the ball went flying and he usually let Dallas go after it.

Dallas wasn't the type to show off, but he was clearly the better player. Both started for the Baker Street Sports Club, Tara knew, but Dallas was the one who handled the ball and shot the best. She also assumed he knew the game the best.

At three Tara stood to go in the house, and when she saw Dallas catch her eye, she signaled for the ball. From the third step of the back porch she launched a shot of about thirty feet, and while it was in the air she decided it would be a sign. If it went through the hoop, that meant everything would be all right. She would get her dad's number, get to talk to him, persuade him to give up his new friend and come back home, and everything would be all right again.

If she missed, then all she could do was hope.

Her shot hit the far side of the rim and bounced high. This time it hit the front of the rim, bounced up to graze the backboard, touched lightly on the back of the rim, and skipped out across the front for a near miss.

"Whoo!" Jimmy shouted. "Almost! What a shot!"

He grabbed the ball and hurled it back to her, just as she was turning to go into the house.

She reached back, caught the pass, and heaved up another shot all in the same motion. This one was right on target, getting nothing but net. She bit her lip to keep from grinning as she spun to go in and heard Jimmy and Dallas cheering the shot.

As fun as it was to show the guys what she could do, however, Tara couldn't shake the thought that she had hinged all her success on that first shot. That was the sign that was to tell her how it would all turn out. She knew it was a silly, childish game and that nothing like that could ever make a real difference in her life. But still, it was hard to keep from feeling that the missed shot really was a sign.

It had been so close, yet it missed. Was that the way it would be with her? Would she come close to getting her dad's number and yet not get it? Would she get permission to see the sky at night from the meadow and for some reason not really get to go? Would she maybe get her father's number and not be able to reach him? Or reach him and not be able to convince him? Or convince him and have her mother refuse to give him another chance?

Would her whole life be just like that shot that had the distance and the angle and the touch, but which was off by a quarter of an inch? A slightly looser or more tightly secured rim might have reacted differently to the bounce and let the ball slip through. But it wasn't to be. All those things had worked together to make an otherwise perfect shot skip away and just miss.

As Tara headed inside to use the upstairs phone, she had a sense of dread, of frustration, of hopelessness. Part of her, that optimistic part that always used to look for the brightest and best in every situation, had left her. As she dialed, she realized that that was one of the differences between how she looked at God and how Dallas and Jimmy seemed to.

To them, God was interested, personally, in everything that happened to them. To her, God was far away. He was in a church, in a book, in a stained-glass window, in a monastery or a seminary. Her hope was in a sign, a long, miraculous basket. Which she had missed.

"Yorty's," Mrs. Yorty said.

"It's me," Tara said. "Suzanne there?"

8

Talking to Jeff

"No," Mrs. Yorty told Tara. "Suzanne called from your house and asked me to have you call her there."

That was just what Tara didn't want to do. How was Suzanne going to tell her her father's new phone number without anyone else hearing? Tara would have to talk to her own mother, which she didn't need or want to do.

She had no choice. She dialed home.

Her little brother, Ray, answered. "Tara!" he said. "When are you coming home? I miss you!"

Tara nearly cried. What a wonderful greeting! She hadn't expected that from anyone, didn't know anyone cared. Her voice was thick with emotion. "I have an open-ended ticket," she said. "That means I can come home tomorrow or next week, whenever."

"So come home tomorrow," Ray said. "I need somebody to talk to."

"About what?"

"You know. All this junk."

"Talk to me now."

"I can't, Tara. Come home soon, please!"

"I'll try, Ray. And thanks."

"You wanna talk to Mom?"

"Is she right there?"

"Uh-huh."

"Put her on."

Tara's conversation with her mother was strained and awkward. Her mother wanted to know why she was calling so soon again, and she said that Jeff wanted to talk to her too. That was bad news for Tara, because that meant that he probably hadn't given her dad's phone number to Suzanne.

"Just checking in," Tara said. "I missed you guys." She was stretching the truth to the limit.

"Well, that's nice," her mother said. "But don't get any ideas about coming home before next weekend. You don't need to come back too long before school starts again."

Tara was silent. This hurt bad. Why didn't her mother want her around? Was it because she was the most talkative about getting the family back together? Or did her mother just not love her anymore? That was too painful to think about, but she couldn't let her mother's comment go unanswered.

"I want to come home, Mom. Ray needs me, and I need you guys."

"Aren't you having fun there?"

"Yeah, but I'd rather be home. Why don't you want me home, Mom?"

"It isn't that I don't want you here, Tara. It's just that I think it's better for you and for us that you are there for spring break."

Tara wanted to shout, to scream, to demand why. She felt unwanted, unloved, in the way. There was so little she could do about her mother and father when she was a two-hour flight from home. What was the point of all this? She knew if she pressed the subject her mother would complain that they had been through it all before.

"OK," Tara muttered. "Let me talk to Jeff."

From the way Jeff spoke, Tara realized that her mother was still standing there, listening. He talked only about news from school, nothing important, nothing that would have been worth telling everyone that he had wanted to talk to Tara when she called.

"I broke fifty-two seconds in the four hundred," he said.

"You're kidding," she said. "What will it take to qualify for the state meet?"

"Oh, I'll probably have to break fifty."

"Probably not this year then," she said.

"Oh, thanks a lot!"

"Well, I just mean that you have only improved about a second and a half since last year, so—"

"But I'm getting bigger and stronger all the time and—"

"Are you still smoking and drinking with your friends?"

There was a long pause and a sigh. "That hasn't hurt me a bit, Tara, and you know it."

"No, I don't. I think it *does* hurt you. I think you should have improved more than you have. You have the size and strength and technique."

"You little know-it-all," he scolded. "Just because you're such a great athlete you think you can tell me how to do it!"

Tara felt terrible. She just cared about Jeff and loved him and didn't want to see him get into trouble or hurt himself. She wanted to apologize, but she didn't want him to think she hadn't meant what she said about the partying. "I'm proud of you, Jeff," she said weakly.

"Yeah, right," he mumbled. "Listen, Mom just left," he said, whispering now. "What do you want Dad's phone number for?"

"Because I want to talk to him—what do you think?"

"What good will that do, Tara?"

"Well, somebody has to try something!"

"Oh, yeah? Well, I tried. I didn't want to believe he really had another woman, but he does, Tara, and you might as well start accepting that."

"I'll never accept that."

"It's true! I met her!"

Tara was quiet. "He introduced you to her?"

"Yup. He tried to convince me that everything was OK. He wanted me to get to know her, to get to like her."

Tara felt a bad taste rise in her throat. It was hard to breathe. Her heart pounded. She didn't want to hear this. But Jeff continued.

"You know what, Tara? She *is* nice. She really is."

Tara could stand it no longer. "OK, so it's true that he's in love with somebody else! I don't have to accept it, and I don't have to like it. I sure don't have to like *her*, and I never will. Who does she think she is, stealing our dad from our mom?"

"Tara," Jeff said. "You can't ever let Mom know that I met this woman."

"Mom doesn't know?"

"Of course not. Dad showed up at school, at the end of track practice, and talked to me by the fence. Offered me a ride home. She was in the car."

"How did he keep Mom from seeing her?"

"He dropped me off at the corner. I told Mom I got a ride home from one of the guys."

"So now you're going to start lying, just like Dad."

"Tara, Dad *is* one of the guys, isn't he? I mean he's a guy, one I know. I wasn't lying!"

"Yeah," Tara spat. "He's one of the guys all right. He's acting like a high school kid."

"You think I'm gonna give you his phone number, knowing how you feel about him?"

"Jeff! I just want to talk to him. Didn't you try to make him see how wrong he was?"

"Not in front of her."

"Well, what's she like? Tell me about her. What's her name?"

"Her name is Sally Graves, and, Tara, you would like her."

Tara could think of nothing better to say than to just snort into the phone. "That'll be the day."

"I'm telling you, Tar', I was surprised. I expected some hard, wicked type. She's young, and she's pretty, and she's very soft-spoken."

"Well, so what? She's ruining our family."

Jeff was quiet for a moment. "Tara," he said finally, "you can't blame this on her. Yeah, she's younger and better looking than Mom. In fact, I've got to tell you something—she looks like a twenty-five-year-old version of you. Short, blond hair, pretty eyes, not as tall as you, but she reminded me of you."

"I don't want to hear that, Jeff."

"But, Tara, this thing wasn't her idea. Dad told me that in front of her, and she didn't argue."

Tara didn't know what to say. What was Jeff trying to do, make this Sally sound good? Innocent?

"She works for Dad, you know," Jeff added.

"I've heard that," Tara said. "So what?"

"Well, she always respected and admired Dad, and then she felt sorry for him when he told her how sad and lonely his marriage was."

"What was he talking about?"

"C'mon, Tara. You know."

"No, I don't! What are *you* talking about?"

"You know how mean Mom can be to Dad, always harping on him about something or other."

"So that gives him the right to find somebody else? He wasn't perfect either, you know."

"All I'm saying is that Dad and Sally fell in love. It wasn't something they meant to do. It just happened. They're happy, and they want us to be happy for them."

"Oh, brother! They're going to have to wait a long time for *me* to be happy. Like forever."

"You need to talk to Dad," Jeff said. "But not to hassle him."

"Then give me his phone number."

"Not when you're feeling like this."

"I'll always feel like this. Now give it to me, or should I get it from Suzanne?"

"Suzanne doesn't have it! I wasn't dumb enough to be tricked into giving it to her."

"Jeff, I'm begging you to give me Dad's number. He tried calling me, so I know he wants to talk to me."

"Tara, I didn't want to tell you this, but he asked me not to give his number to anyone."

"Not even to me?"

"Especially you."

"He said that?"

"He mentioned you by name, yes. If he wants to talk to you, he'll call again."

"Jeff!"

"What?"

"You're serious? You're not going to give me the number?"

"Sorry, Tar'."

"I hate you!"

"Oh, that persuaded me."

"I hate you, Jeff, and I don't care if I ever see you again! You don't care about me, and you don't care about Mom or Dad or our family!"

Click.

Tara couldn't believe it when Jeff hung up on her. She was tempted to call back and scream at somebody or talk to Suzanne, but she was too mad. She threw herself onto the bed and sobbed into the pillow.

Her mother didn't want her home. Her father didn't want to talk to her. Her little brother cared and missed her, but he couldn't help. In fact, *she* needed to help *him*. But she was helpless. What could she do? She had nowhere to turn.

Tara felt a desperate urge to pray, but she didn't know how to start or what to say. "God," she began, "I'll do anything if You'll—" But what? What did she want Him to do? Did she want Him to miraculously put it all back together? Or did she want His help in trying to fix it herself? She felt so tiny, so worthless, so meaningless.

She realized that as much as she wanted her parents' marriage put back together, she also wanted them both to care about her and love her the way she always believed that they had.

She wanted somebody to love her, and that—she suddenly realized—was what she wanted from God. "I'll do anything," she sobbed again. But she didn't know where to go from there. She would do anything if God would just—what?

"If You'll just love me!" she blurted. "I want You to love me!"

9

The Night Sky

What Tara didn't know how to say was that she wanted God to talk to her, to reach out to her, to show Himself to her in some way. She didn't know if her parents would ever get back together, but she sure wanted to know that God cared about her.

That night after dinner she borrowed Amy's bike and rode with Dallas to Jimmy's. She hoped neither Dallas nor Jimmy would notice how quiet she was. No one had said anything at dinner about her red face and puffy eyes from crying most of the afternoon. She wondered what they would have thought if they had known she had even tried praying.

Dallas whistled loudly as they skidded to a stop behind Jimmy's back door. Star Diamond snorted and trotted to the fence. Dallas left Tara and went to pet the big horse.

Jimmy came out smiling, shaking a brown paper bag. "Popcorn!" he said. "Enough for all of us."

That sounded good, but Tara wished it made her happier. She was still down, flat, and unable to be good company. She liked her cousin, and she enjoyed Jimmy, and she didn't want to be a drag.

"Do we hafta run up the hill again?" Jimmy asked as they joined Dallas.

"Nah," Dallas said. "Unless either of you wants to."

They both shook their heads, and the three started out, walking slowly over the same path they had run that morning. The sky was clear and black, but Tara had vowed not to look up until they were in the same place in the meadow. Her mind was full of the memory of the blueness that had surrounded her that morning, and though it had almost scared her with its beauty and overwhelming hugeness, she knew the feeling would be even more powerful at night.

As they reached the top of the hill in the meadow, Tara shivered with excitement. She was still hurt, still sad, still frustrated at not being able to talk with her dad. But she had to admit she might even enjoy this. The popcorn smelled good. The boys were people she liked a lot. And as they moved down the other side of the hill, no light was visible anywhere.

The lights from the small Calabresi farm were hidden now. Jimmy had been chattering about something, but just as Tara hoped, he fell silent. They sat in the cold, dewy grass. All Tara heard was the rustling of the popcorn as Jimmy set the bag aside. Her eyes slowly became used to the lower light as she and the boys sat in almost pitch darkness.

The moon rode low on the horizon and was a mere sliver. Tara closed her eyes and lowered herself onto her back, put her hands behind her head, and lay there for a moment not moving. She kept her eyes closed and became aware of her breathing, of her heartbeat. She hoped Dallas and Jimmy wouldn't act like typical boys and feel they needed to comment on the beauty of the night or the sky.

When she was ready, she slowly opened her eyes, and it was she who couldn't keep from exclaiming, "Wow!"

One of the boys shushed her, and she was sorry she had said anything. But she couldn't help herself. It was too much, too beautiful, too majestic—too— too—too something she couldn't even think of.

Her entire field of vision was filled with bright, shining, twinkly, fiery stars, set against a deep blue, inky near-blackness that stretched as far as she could see. At first the stars appeared to be all the same distance away, though some seemed larger than others. Then she sensed their distances, not in any real, knowing way, but getting a three-dimensional picture of them. If some looked miles away, others looked hundreds of miles away, though she knew from her study of the stars and planets that in fact they were light years, hundreds of thousands and millions and even billions of miles away.

She knew that some of these tiny dots of light were in fact many times larger than the earth and even the sun. Some were brighter than the sun but were so far away that they looked like wee specks of light. The hardest thing for her to grasp was that it took the light from some of those stars so long to reach the earth that the star could explode and send a shower of fireworks into the heavens and she might not see it happen until days later. The occasional shooting star she saw deep in the heavens may have happened yesterday or even a week before.

Tara was nearly crushed with the astonishing beauty and scope of the creation. Yes, that's what it was. The work of God. She had asked Him to love her, to somehow reveal Himself to her. Was that what this was? How could she grasp Him, connect with Him, understand what He was all about by simply staring into His world?

She hadn't heard any movement, no pages turning, but suddenly, in the dark stillness, with the damp ground making her shiver, Tara saw the faint light of Dallas's flashlight and heard him begin reading again from his Bible.

"When I look up into the night skies and see the work of your fingers—the moon and the stars you have made—I cannot understand how you can bother with mere puny man, to pay any attention to him."

Tara hoped Dallas would not go on, would read no more until what she had just heard sunk in and made sense to her. And as if he has been reading her mind, Dallas read it again.

Is that ever the truth! she thought. *God, how can You care? How can You pay any attention to me? I'm just a girl, just a little person out of millions of people. My problems are big to me, but what do they mean to Someone who made the moon and stars, the earth, the galaxies, the universe?*

And Dallas read on. "And yet you have made him only a little lower than the angels, and placed a crown of glory and honor upon his head. You have put him in charge of everything you made; everything is put under his authority: all sheep and oxen, and wild animals too, the birds and fish, and all the life in the sea. O Jehovah, our Lord, the majesty and glory of your name fills the earth."

Tara was full of questions. But first she wanted to hear that again, all of it. She asked Dallas to read it from the beginning. He didn't answer. He just started in. As she looked into the sky she believed with all her heart that those words were written by someone who knew the God who had created all this. There was no doubt in her mind that what Dallas was reading was about this very Person.

"What does it mean," she asked, "where it says he has put a crown on man's head?"

"I think it means that he has honored us," Dallas said. "Even though we can't imagine how the Creator could care about us, because we're so small and seem so meaningless or worthless, he put us in charge of everything he made. So He does care. He does love us. He *is* interested in us. And that's why I think He wants us to be devoted to Him, to love Him, to talk to Him."

They sat in silence for a while before Jimmy grunted as he reached for his popcorn bag and offered it to Dallas and Tara. Dallas took a huge handful, then said, "I'm sorry, Tara. I should have let you go first."

She waved him off and took a handful herself. Maybe it was where she was or who she was with or what she was thinking about, but popcorn had never tasted so delicious to her. It was still only slightly warm, but the buttery, salty flavor of the corn was wonderful. She took more and more until she wished someone had thought to bring something to drink.

Jimmy shook the bag. Only a few unpopped kernels were left. He smacked his lips. "I could sure use something to drink," he said. "Should I go get us something?"

"That would be great," Tara said. "Thanks."

Jimmy hurried away.

"Are you as thirsty as I am?" Tara asked Dallas.

He nodded. "There's a verse about being thirsty too," he said. "You wanna hear it?"

Tara never thought she'd ask anybody to read her more from the Bible, but she nodded. Nothing seemed more right just then.

Dallas looked in the back of his Bible. "I know it's in Psalms too, but I don't know exactly where it is—ah, here we go. Psalm forty-two."

He flipped back and began reading, "As the deer pants for water, so I long for you, O God. I thirst for God, the living God. Where can I find him to come and stand before him? Day and night I weep for his help."

Tara shook her head. "I don't understand how that book can say so much in so few words. It was as if it was written just for me."

"In a way, it was," Dallas said. "You want to hear the end of that psalm? It ends good."

"Sure."

"But O my soul, don't be discouraged. Don't be upset. Expect God to act! For I know that I shall again have plenty of reason to praise him for all that he will do. He is my help! He is my God!"

Tara was suddenly overcome with emotion. She realized that she was thirsty for God. She hungered for Him. She had prayed for His help. She wanted His love. She wanted to know Him as a person, not as a religious character, someone she heard about or read about. She wanted Him, and she was thirstier inside for Him than she ever could be for something to drink.

She didn't know how Dallas knew so well when to say something, when to read something, and when to just be quiet. Now, when she needed stillness, he said nothing. She lay back and gazed at the stars again, wondering once more how God could care about such a tiny dot like her on the earth.

But she was drawn to Him. She wanted Him. She was jealous of Dallas and Jimmy because they seemed to really know Him. It was no longer puzzling to her that they should be devoted to Him and want to show it. How could that be? How could she have changed her mind about God so suddenly and so completely?

Would she have the nerve to tell Dallas? Could she form the words on her lips and say, "I need God. I want to know God. How can I know Him?"

Her embarrassment melted away. Maybe it was because they were in the darkness and she knew he couldn't see her clearly, but she was ready to tell him. She wanted to know God the way Dallas knew Him, and if that meant risking some weak, uncertain part of her, she would do it. She sat up and faced Dallas. He looked at her. And the bell rang from the back door of the Calabresi place.

Dallas jumped up and scampered over the top of the hill. "My ma doesn't want me bringin' bottles up there!" Jimmy bellowed. "She wants us to have it down here, in the house!"

"We'll be right there!" Dallas called back. "Give us a few minutes!"

How did he know she needed a few more minutes? Tara was constantly astonished at her cousin. How could anybody that young, and a boy at that, be so sensitive?

"Dallas," she said, "I need to talk to you."

"I know," he said.

"About something real important."

He nodded. "I know."

"Well, if you know so much," she said, "why don't you tell me what I want to talk about?"

"No," he said, smiling. "That has to come from you."

10
The Decision

Tara felt as if she were on the edge of a cliff. She had the feeling that she was about to make a decision she would remember all her life. She felt more grown up, more adult than ever. As much as she wanted to know God the way Dallas knew Him, the words stuck in her throat.

That was what she wanted to say. It was all she wanted to say. Just, "I want to know God the way you know Him."

So why couldn't she say it? She knew that Dallas knew what she wanted, so why couldn't he help her out? Why couldn't Dallas say it for her? There was no doubt in her mind that he really did know exactly what she was thinking, so there must be some reason that he was forcing her to say it for herself.

She was afraid that if she spoke she would burst into tears before she was able to say what she wanted and needed to say. She hoped, she wished, she prayed Dallas would just say it for her. But he did not.

She looked down, but she couldn't see the grass she felt with her finger tips. She opened her mouth to speak but couldn't coax the words out. She took a deep breath and let it out, then sniffed self-consciously.

Maybe if I whisper it, she thought. *But why does this have to be so hard? Dallas knows what I want to say, and if God is God, He knows too.*

Dallas seemed to sit patiently, though the silence was eternal to Tara. She began to fear that Jimmy would lose patience, would ring the bell again, or holler at them, or, worse, that he would come looking for them. Then the moment would be lost. As scared as she was, as nervous as she was, as shy as she was about telling what was on her mind, she knew that she was as close as she would ever be to knowing God. If she let this moment pass, she sensed, she might never come back to it.

If it was embarrassing and difficult to do this with her cousin, how much worse would it be if she was back home, back in the middle of that trouble? How much worse would it be if she had to explain herself to her mother or her older brother or her best friend?.

She whispered so quietly that she could hardly hear herself, "I want to know God."

Dallas said nothing. Had he not heard her? Surely he had heard her. Was he making this more difficult on purpose? Why would he want to do that? She couldn't make herself repeat it. She looked up, searching for his face, his eyes, in the darkness. When he didn't move or speak, she shivered.

"Did you hear me, Dallas?" she asked, almost angry.

"I heard you," he said simply. "But you're talking to the wrong person."

"What do you mean?"

"Tell *Him,*" he said.

"I don't know what to say."

"You want to know Him like a friend, so talk to Him like a friend. What good is it to know Him if you can't talk to Him the same way you talk to me?"

"It wasn't easy to tell you what I just told you, and you're my favorite cousin."

"What were you afraid of? You knew I'd understand."

"I know. Maybe I wasn't afraid. Maybe I just hate to admit that I need anything or anyone, and I don't even want you to know it."

Dallas nodded but said nothing.

"So, what do I say to Him?" Tara asked again.

"I don't know," he said. "What do you want to tell Him?"

"That I need Him. That I want to know Him. That I don't know how to do this."

"I think that's a good place to start. Do you want to be alone?"

She hadn't thought of that, but yes, maybe that was what she needed. If she was going to talk to God, to get serious about Him, maybe she needed to do it on her own. She shrugged, then reluctantly nodded. "Yes, maybe that would be good."

"Let me tell you two things before I go," Dallas said, standing. "First, because God is perfect and we're not, we can't come to Him by ourselves. That's why we talked about 'coming to Christ.' He's the only way to God. You know why?"

"I know He died for the sins of the world. I've heard that all my life."

"But right now the sins of the world are not keeping you from God."

"What is?"

"Your own sin."

That sounded too blunt, too hard for Tara. She knew she wasn't perfect. Who was? "Am I any worse than anyone else?" she said.

"That's just it," Dallas said. "We've all sinned. None of us can stand alone before God. Jesus is the only way to Him, and He said so when He said, 'I am the way, and the truth, and the life. No man comes to the Father but by Me.'"

Tara was confused. "What does it mean?"

"It means that to know God you have to come to Christ. Through Christ. If you receive Christ, He gives you the power to become a child of God."

Tara's head was spinning. How would she ever learn all this? How could someone not even a year older than she know all this? Wasn't she starting too late, too far behind her cousin?

Dallas continued. "God loves us and wants us to know Him, but something has to be done about the sin that keeps us from Him. How can we be friends with a perfect God?"

That was what Tara wanted to know. Dallas was making it sound impossible. "I'm listening," she said.

"Jesus already did it," he said. "He took our punishment, and all we have to do is believe in Him and receive Him."

"I believe in Him!" Tara insisted. "How do I receive Him?"

"You're still thirsty for God?"

"Yes."

"One more verse I want to read you, and then you're on your own. This is from the New Testament, John seven thirty-seven and thirty-eight. Jesus says, 'If anyone is thirsty, let him come to me and drink. For the Scriptures declare that rivers of living water shall flow from the inmost being of anyone who believes in me.'"

Dallas began to move away.

"Dallas," Tara said simply.

He stopped and turned around.

"Don't leave me not knowing how to do this. I don't want to get this close to getting serious about God and do it wrong."

"You're not going to do it wrong, Tara. If you tell God what you've told me, it will be more than enough. You want to know Him. You know you're separated from Him, and you know why. Come to Jesus to get to God."

"I just tell Him that?"

Dallas nodded.

"And what will happen to me?"

"Nothing will happen to you except that God will give you what you ask for."

"How will I know?"

"You know what, Tara? I don't know how you'll know, because I was so young when I received Christ that I don't remember how it felt. I don't remember feeling any different. I've talked to people who feel wonderful or forgiven or complete or whatever. But even if you don't feel *anything*, you have to know that God loves you enough to give you the gift He promises you."

She nodded, but asked, "The gift?"

"You will know God, like you said you wanted. But the gift is Jesus. He's the One who made it possible for us to know God, so He's the way *and* the gift. We get to be with God someday because of what Jesus did for us."

"But I need to know —"

Dallas held up a hand. "Tara, I'm sorry. I have told you all I know. I can't convince you or push you or make you do anything. You said you wanted to know God, and I'm telling you that Jesus is the only way. You can talk to God the way you talk to me."

Without another word, Dallas moved up to the top of the hill and down the other side.

Tara felt alone, terribly alone. She was scared, not of the dark, not of the night, not of anything in the meadow. She knew where Dallas would be, and she could follow him to Jimmy's if she wanted.

She was afraid of what this all meant. She didn't know or understand much about God and Jesus and the Bible, but she knew this was the right thing to do. Rather than making her feel grown up and wise, this whole decision made her feel small and full of questions.

Tara didn't know whether to kneel or fold her hands or close her eyes. That was what she remembered reading about —and seeing pictures of—when she thought of praying. But if God was out there somewhere, and if she could talk to Him like a friend, she could speak out loud. She could keep her eyes open. She could lie down and see what He had made.

And so she did. She lay back carefully and looked at the stars and the moon, which was now a little higher in the sky and which allowed her to be aware of more shadows and shapes around her.

"God," she began. "I believe in You. I believe You made all this and that You are here. I believe You made me and care about me and love me. I love You and want to know you, to be your child, like Dallas said. God, I'm thirsty for You. I know I don't deserve You and that I need You to forgive me. Please forgive me. You're offering me a gift. I don't know how to receive Jesus except to say that I'll take Him."

Tara found herself lifting her arms toward the sky, as if to receive Jesus from God. "Thank you, God," she said. "I promise to learn everything I can about You and read the Bible and talk to You everyday."

She didn't know what else to say. She let her arms fall and folded them across her chest. She didn't expect lightning or thunder or a warm feeling inside. She just kept staring at the stars. Then it hit her. She realized that she had not asked God for anything for herself except to know Him. She had not pleaded that He put her parents back together. She had not asked that she become happy. She had simply received His gift of love.

Tara didn't know how long she stayed in the meadow, but when she stood her back was wet where the dew had soaked through her jacket and top. She shivered as the breeze hit her. Looking around at the grove of the trees below, the tops of the pines yellow from the moon, she knew she would never forget this place. She would want to come back here many times.

Tara turned and moved slowly over the crest of the hill. There, waiting at the bottom, was Dallas. He was staring into the distance, the other way, toward the house. When she neared the bottom he turned and saw her. Tara approached him quickly and did something she hadn't done since she was a preschooler and her parents made her. She hugged him.

Dallas seemed too surprised and embarrassed to hug her back, and when she pulled away he looked at her, as if to say, "Well?"

"Dallas," she said, "I need something to drink."

He nodded and slowly turned toward the house. So, he wasn't going to ask her, she realized. "I mean, I'm *really* thirsty," she added.

He nodded again. "Me, too."

Tara couldn't make him ask what had happened. It had been so personal, so special, that she wouldn't have wanted to tell him everything anyway. But she wanted him to know, and since he was the one who had explained it to her, he deserved to know.

"Dallas," she said, stopping.

He turned and looked at her.

"I'm only thirsty because of the popcorn."

"I know," he said. "Me too."

"I'm not thirsty for God anymore."

He stared at her. "You're not?"

"No, and I never will be again."

"You received Christ?"

She nodded.

This time he hugged her.

GATE
7
SAIR

11
Heading Home

By the time Tara was driven to the airport a week later, she felt as if she had lived her entire life again. First, going to church with the O'Neils was different than she had ever remembered from her church or theirs. Every word of every song seemed new and fresh and meaningful to her. She didn't daydream during prayers but prayed along. She didn't tune out the sermon either, not understanding all of it but listening carefully.

She enjoyed the reactions of Jimmy and especially Aunt Bev when they learned that she had received Christ. She even told her little cousins, who told her that they had done the same. Dallas's dad, her Uncle Dale, had returned from the road on Monday, and he had prayed with her. It was one of the most special times of her life.

At dinner that night, he had thanked God for welcoming her into His family. She was warm all over and felt close to these relatives who were Christians just as she was. Tara was beginning to understand what it meant to be part of the family of God.

On her every-other-day phone call home, she was nicer to her mother and didn't push Jeff to give her her father's new phone number. She still wanted to talk to him, more desperately than ever. But in her daily Bible reading and prayer—once with Dallas and Jimmy, once with just Dallas, several times with the family, and the rest by herself—she was learning the best thing she could do for her parents: love them.

She hated what her father was doing, and she hated how her mother was reacting to it. She wanted them back together, but more than anything she wanted them to come to Christ. She chuckled to herself when she first realized she had said that. The phrase had sounded so strange to her when she'd first heard it. It had been like a foreign language to her.

Now her goal was to talk to her brothers and parents and Suzanne about what was most important in her life. She believed that if they would become true Christians, people with Christ in their lives, it would help them solve their other problems.

The hardest thing for Tara to do, especially during that first week of her new friendship with God, was to learn some things from the Bible that seemed very strange to her. Uncle Dale led her through a brief study one night on what he called the paradoxes of the Bible. She had heard the word before, but she needed him to explain it again.

"A paradox is something that doesn't seem to make sense. People say they want to be somebody special. Jesus says that if you want to be great, you serve other people. To be special, you become humble. People want all the money they can get. Jesus says that the richest people are those who give to others. People say they want to get revenge on their enemies, to defeat them, to get even with them. Jesus says to love your enemies and pray for those who use you."

Tara sat shaking her head. "I'm supposed to love Sally Graves?" she said.

"Who's Sally Graves?" Uncle Dale said.

Tara told him, and he didn't say much. "You know, Tara, I think the fewer people who know the details of all that, the better. I'm praying for your dad that he will see what he is doing is wrong and that he'll come back to your mother. If that happens, he doesn't need to be embarrassed that I know all about the woman he was involved with. So, don't tell me any more details. Just let me say this. If this woman is your enemy, if she has hurt you, then the Bible says you must love her and pray for her."

"What do I pray? I'd like to pray that something bad will happen to her."

"You pray that God will have His way in her life. Do you think that would mean hurting or killing her?"

"I don't know, but I know He can't like what she's doing."

"True, but you'll find as you keep studying the Bible that God loves everybody. He hates sin, but He loves sinners. We should be glad for that. We may not have ever done what this Sally Graves is doing, but we don't deserve any better treatment from God than she does."

"So I should pray that she becomes a Christian?"

"Of course! What better thing could happen?"

Tara almost laughed. "Imagine how Dad would like it if his new girl friend became a Christian! She couldn't be his girl friend anymore, could she?"

Uncle Dale shook his head. "Not and be pleasing to God."

"Then that's what I'm going to pray for," she said. "In fact, I'm going to pray for her and my parents and my brothers and Suzanne. I can't wait to talk to them about this."

Uncle Dale was not smiling. "You know, Tara, we love you, and we worry about you. Frankly, your Aunt Bev and I are a little concerned about how your parents, particularly your mother, will react to this."

Aunt Bev, who had been in the kitchen, joined Tara and Uncle Dale in the living room. "He's right," her aunt said. "I know my sister, and she's not too excited about how serious we are about our faith in God."

"I didn't know that," Tara said. "I mean she said you were too religious or something, but I guess I didn't know she knew that much about it. I'll be surprised if she still feels that way after I explain it to her and tell her how close I feel to God."

"That's a problem," her uncle said. "The Bible makes it clear that God wants us to tell others about Him, but telling your mother is going to be very difficult."

"That's right," Aunt Bev said. "You see, I have already told your mother all she needs to know to become a Christian. She doesn't want to hear any more about it, and she's going to assume that as soon as we got you here, we forced God down your throat."

"But you didn't! I could tell how much He meant to you, but no one pressured or pushed me!"

Uncle Dale and Aunt Bev looked at each other. "I guess what we're trying to say, hon," Tara's aunt said, "is that we want to be careful of two things. First, we all know that you came to Christ on your own. But your mother is not going to believe that, and we want to be careful not to conspire against her. Do you know what that means?"

Tara nodded. "We shouldn't look like we're doing something behind her back."

"Right. And the second thing is, you want to be very careful how you tell her what has happened to you."

"How do I do that?"

"Maybe," her uncle said, "you let your actions do the talking. You've always been a nice, sweet girl around here, but even we have noticed a change in you since you've become a Christian. It's not a new language or that you're always praying or carrying a Bible. You're a different person, and it shows. If your mother was ignorant of how to become a Christian, we would encourage you to tell her right away. But since she knows, probably the best thing for you to do is to say nothing. Just live out the love of Christ at home."

"How do I do that?"

"If your faith is genuine, you won't even have to think about it. Just remember that you are representing God now.

People who notice the new you will soon ask what's different about you. Then you can tell them in a nice way."

"My mother doesn't even notice me anymore. I'm in the way."

"You can imagine how much she has on her mind with her marriage in trouble."

Tara nodded. "So my job is to pray and be nice."

Uncle Dale laughed. "That's about the size of it. And knowing you, you'd rather do something dramatic to move things along."

"Well, I still want to talk to my dad, if that's what you mean."

"You have to be very careful about that, too," Aunt Bev said. "I would go very slowly and don't push. The longer he goes without talking to you, the more guilty he will feel. He'll eventually get in touch with you."

"But I need to talk to him soon to get him to come back home!"

"You'd better leave that to God. He needs to know how much he's hurting you, yes, but don't assume you can fix everything by yourself. You don't have to do that anymore. You have God now."

"Will God fix everything?"

"There's no guarantee. He will take care of you. That's a promise. No matter what happens, He'll always be there for you."

Somehow, Tara understood. She had not come to Christ, not become a child of God, only to have all her problems solved. She wanted God to work in her family. She wanted her parents to get back together. She wanted them to love each other and to love her. But most of all, she wanted them to love God as she did.

She would pray for them all, and she would follow the advice of her aunt and uncle and just ask God to help make her a good daughter to her mother. Sure, she wished her mother wouldn't treat her as if she was in the way, but then maybe Tara hadn't proved that she could be a friend to her mother either.

How could she help a mother who had been cheated, abandoned, disgraced by her husband's moving in with a younger woman? Tara didn't pretend to know what to do or say about that. But she would be whatever she could be for her mother. She would help her, listen to her, be nice to her, not fight with her, not badger her.

Neither would she try to beat her mother over the head with her newfound faith in Christ. Uncle Dale was right about that. Her best chance with her mother was to show her a new daughter. It might take a long time, but it was the only right thing to do. She would begin looking for other Christians to spend time with, something Dallas had recommended. And while she would not try to get permission to go to another, better church, one where people believed in a personal God like she did, she would try to get as much out of her church as possible.

As Tara hugged the O'Neils at the airport, Aunt Bev slipped a new Bible into her carry-on bag. She couldn't wait to start reading it on the plane. When she boarded, she had plans. Plans to talk to her father. Plans even to talk to his new girl friend. But mostly she would pray. She wanted to see the people in her life know what it felt like to be loved by God.

Even if nothing else happened, if nothing else changed, she would hope and pray for that. That would be more than enough.

Moody Press, a ministry of the Moody Bible Institute,
is designed for education, evangelization, and edification.
If we may assist you in knowing more about Christ
and the Christian life, please write us without obligation:
Moody Press, c/o MLM, Chicago, Illinois 60610.